Dino-Daddy

Mark Sperring

Illustrated by Sam Lloyd

BLOOMSBURY

LONDON NEW DELHI NEW YORK SYDNEY

There's someone here at home
who's lots of dino-fun.

And you'd never EVER swap him
for another dino-one . . .

He's really rather useful
for lots of dino-things.

Like blowing up balloons

Bang

POP

And tying them on strings!

The park would NEVER be such fun without him standing by.

No one can spin you faster –

Weeee!!

or swing you
quite so high . . .

And though he has a list of jobs he has to dino-do,

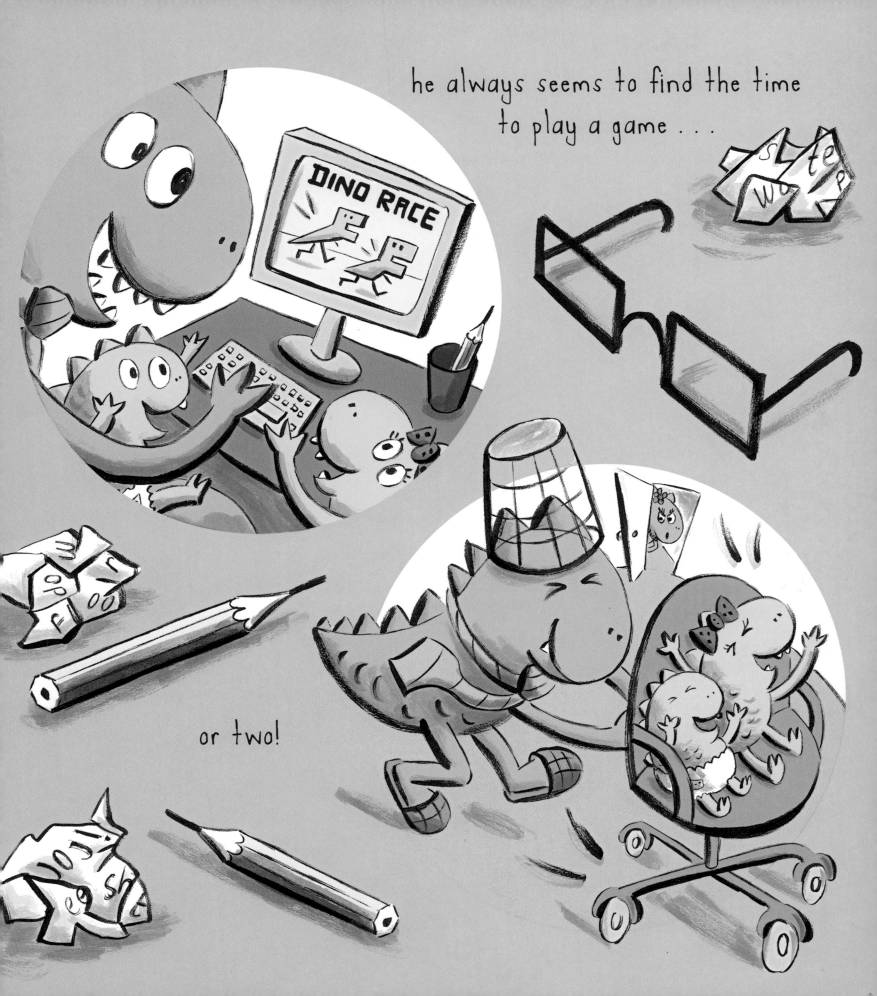

he always seems to find the time
to play a game . . .

or two!

He's a dino-tastic builder, watch him drive that dino-crane.

He can build the tallest towers . . .

CRASH!

and stack them up again.

And even when he takes a nap,

he joins in with
the fun . . .

he's your dino Sleeping Beauty . . .

He can turn into a monster
and cause a
FRIGHTFUL scene!

ARGG!

Quick, run, HE'S DINO-DEADLY . . .

Yes, he's a
rough-and-tumble dino,

he's the
play-mat-wrestling-king.

He can be your circus pony
clip-clopping round the ring.

He can wow you with his magic —

HUH?

Where did that cake all go?

Dino-Daddy, take a bow, please . . .

For G and H ~ MS

For Ian . . . a Dino-Daddy dude xxx ~ SL

Bloomsbury Publishing, London, New Delhi, New York and Sydney
First published in Great Britain in 2015 by Bloomsbury Publishing Plc
50 Bedford Square, London, WC1B 3DP

Text copyright © Mark Sperring 2015
Illustrations copyright © Sam Lloyd 2015
The moral rights of the author and illustrator have been asserted

A CIP catalogue record of this book is available from the British Library

ISBN 978 1 4088 4969 9 (HB)
ISBN 978 1 4088 4970 5 (PB)

Printed in China by Leo Paper Products, Heshan, Guangdong

1 3 5 7 9 10 8 6 4 2

www.bloomsbury.com

All papers used by Bloomsbury Publishing are natural, recyclable products
made from wood grown in well-managed forests.
The manufacturing processes conform to the environmental regulations of the country of origin

BLOOMSBURY is a registered trademark of Bloomsbury Publishing Plc